ATTACK OF THE ALIEN DUNG!

For Ida Davies McCarty, who will one day save the world!
- GPJ

For Mum, Jackie and Andy, for unstinting
support and encouragement
- SM

STRIPES PUBLISHING
An imprint of the Little Tiger Group
1 The Coda Centre, 189 Munster Road,
London SW6 6AW

A paperback original
First published in Great Britain in 2017

Text copyright © Gareth P. Jones, 2017
Illustrations copyright © Steve May, 2017

ISBN: 978-1-84715-779-9

GARETH P. JONES

ILLUSTRATED BY

STEVE MAY

Stripes

PET DEFENDERS

Protecting those who protect us

Did you know that Earth is under constant alien attack?

Don't worry.

We are the Pet Defenders, a secret society of domestic animals. We are your dogs, cats, rabbits and rodents. While you are off at school or work or doing whatever it is you humans do, we are keeping the Earth safe.

We keep our work hidden because we know what humans are like. The first sight of a yellow-bellied three-armed Flobber-Dobber with an electrocuting bottom and you'll panic.

TOP SECRET

Before you know it, you'll have blown up the very planet we're trying to defend.

Just carry on as normal — stroke your cats, take your dogs for walks and clean out your hamster cages. Don't forget to feed us, but please … let *us* take care of the aliens.

Now that you know all this, we need you to forget it. Our specially trained seagulls will take care of that. Ah, here they are with the Forget-Me-Plop now…

SSSPLAT!

DOGFINGER

CHAPTER 1

A RUDE AWAKENING

Tap, tap, tap.

Biskit opened an eye and lifted the ear that had been covering it. The morning sunlight was blinding. He flopped his ear over again and tried to get back to sleep.

"Go away," he mumbled.

Tap, tap, tap.

This time he opened both eyes and lifted both ears. The sun had risen over the rooftops and was shining directly on his dog basket. A seagull stood on the window ledge. Seeing Biskit, it tipped its head to one side.

"Leave me alone," said Biskit.

The seagull looked at him blankly.

"Come on, Biskit! It's too early for barking!" shouted Philip from his bedroom.

"See what you've done now, you dumb bird," whispered Biskit. "You've woken up my owner."

The seagull was about to *tap, tap, tap* on the window again, so Biskit nudged it open with his nose. A cold winter's breeze made his straggly brown fur stand on end.

The seagull hopped into the room, looked around, then squawked.

"BISKIT!" yelled Philip.

"Quiet," snarled Biskit.

"Agent Biskit," said a voice from a speaker attached to the seagull's leg.

"Commander F," said Biskit, recognizing the gruff tone of his grumpy rabbit boss.

"This is the second seagull I've sent, you mangy mutt. Report to my Hutch Quarters now."

"But it's my day off, sir," said Biskit. "My owner's taking me to see that new Danger Dog film."

There was no reply from the speaker. Biskit stared at the seagull and waited.

The seagull stared back. **Squawk!**

"The commander's gone, hasn't he?" said Biskit.

The seagull turned to leave. As it spread its wings, it knocked a photo off the windowsill. Biskit sprang up and snatched the photo mid-air. He landed with a thud in the corner of the room.

"Ow," he groaned.

He placed the picture down in front of him. It was a photograph of him on the beach with Philip's ex-girlfriend, Susie. She was walking along while Biskit ran on ahead. Biskit was gazing at it, remembering the day fondly, when he noticed a burning sensation coming from his bottom. He looked round and realized he had landed on the heater.

"**Hot! Hot! Hot!**" barked Biskit.

"Right. That's it." He could hear Philip opening his bedroom door and padding down the corridor in his slippers.

Biskit had no choice. He had been looking forward to spending some quality owner-pet time with Philip, but the Pet Defenders needed him. He dashed out of the room and straight through the dog flap.

"BISKIT?" Philip called after his dog, but he knew there was no point. Biskit would come back when he was good and ready. He went into the living room and picked up the photograph, which he returned to its place on the sill. He sighed and closed the window. He paused to look at the seagull standing on the roof across the road. For a moment Philip felt as though the seagull was watching him, but then the bird flew away and he went back to bed.

CHAPTER 2

COMMANDER F

To the people who lived there, Nothington-on-Sea was an ordinary seaside town. To the Pet Defenders, it was a hub of alien activity. In the summer months, human tourists liked its pebble beach and fish & chip shops. Its alien visitors were less fussy about the seasons.

Biskit ran through backyards and down backstreets and back alleys before slipping under a wooden fence into the back garden where Commander F lived. He jumped over a flower bed and peered into the hutch. It was empty. Biskit sniffed the air. The rabbit was close.

"Commander F, are you th— Oof." Something white, fluffy and extremely heavy landed on Biskit's back. "That hurt," he complained.

"Aww. Did the little fluffy bunny hurt the poor doggy?" Commander F's gruff voice dripped with sarcasm.

"Little? That pregnant Moon Hippo weighed less than you," exclaimed Biskit.

"Watch it," Commander F snarled. "Emily has had me on a carrot-only diet all week and I get grouchy when I'm hungry."

"What's got your tail in a twist, anyway?" asked Biskit, wishing he was still tucked up asleep in his nice warm dog basket.

Commander F climbed off Biskit's back and hopped round to face him. "What's got my tail in a twist? I'll tell you, Biskit, me old mongrel mucker – yesterday afternoon in the middle of town there was an unexpected downpour—"

"You can hardly blame me for the weather," interrupted Biskit.

"Of pepper," continued Commander F. "Do you know what happens when it rains pepper, Biskit?"

"People sneeze?"

Commander F snarled.

"When it rains pepper, people ask questions.

Questions such as, *Why is it raining pepper?*"

"Yes, well. About that…" Biskit sniffed a flower patch, picking up the scents of all the animals that had visited recently. "It turned out that last lot of giant alien invaders weren't an army after all. They were a highly trained catering squad."

"Catering?"

"Cooks, sir. Planet chefs. They wanted to grill the Earth on its own sun. Apparently globe cooking is all the rage in the enormiverse."

Commander F sniffed at a pile of carrots before selecting one. He bit the end off and spat it out. "So how did you get rid of them?"

"I convinced them that the planet wasn't ripe yet. Too green, you see, sir. They were gone by nightfall."

"Hmm." Commander F snorted. "So the pepper rain?"

"That was to make us taste better. Apparently this part of the galaxy lacks flavour."

The large white rabbit scowled at his carrot then took a nibble. "Biskit, you're a good agent…"

"Thanks," said Biskit.

"But you're too careless. You're irresponsible and you never think things thr—"

"Not thinking things through is what I do best, sir."

"Stop interrupting me. As you know, Earth is under constant attack from aliens, and it is our job to send them back to where they came from. But we also need to stop the humans from finding out what's going on. We had to Forget-Me-Plop half the town after that pepper storm yesterday."

"So? Isn't that why we have seagulls carrying Forget-Me-Plop?" said Biskit. "What's the problem?"

16

"Your attitude is the problem. I'm assigning you a new partner. As soon as I can find someone willing to work with you, that is."

"Sorry, sir, I work alone now," said Biskit firmly.

Commander F's voice softened. "Listen, I know you feel bad about what happened to your last partner."

Biskit bristled. "Champ was a good dog and a dedicated agent, but he knew the risks when he took the job," he said defensively.

"He also knew the rules… Unlike you, you canine catastrophe," said Commander F. "Do you have any idea how many witnesses saw that pepper rain?"

"You worry too much, Fluffikins."

"That's Commander F to you." The bunny hopped into his hutch and took another bite of carrot. "Only my owner gets to use my given name."

"How is Emily?" asked Biskit.

"She's the one who put me on this diet. She should spend more time doing her maths homework and less time worrying about my weight, if you ask me," he grumbled. "What about Philip? Still pining after Susie?"

"Yes, I was hoping to cheer him up with a trip to the cinema…"

"Well, that will have to wait. We've had a report of unusual activity at Clifftop Farm from one of the cows."

"A cow!" exclaimed Biskit. "The last time we had a report from a cow it was about a mysterious cloud with legs. Do you know what it turned out to be? A sheep."

"That's as may be," said Commander F, "but we've got to chase up all leads, investigate all threats. The NERDS are already up there. So forget about your silly film and get to that farm before I show you why they used to call me Thumper!"

CHAPTER 3

A DUNG-SPOTTING COW

On a good day Clifftop Farm boasted beautiful views across the bay, but by the time Biskit made it up there, the sky had clouded over and the wind was picking up. Not that Biskit would be spending much time admiring the view anyway – he hated heights. He slipped under a gate into the field, keeping as far away from the edge of the cliff as possible.

A cow nodded at Biskit, then said, "Oh, hellooo, daaarling."

"Hello, madam. I am Agent Biskit of the Pet Defenders." In Biskit's experience, cows were not the brightest of animals, so he spoke in a loud, clear voice.

"Why are you shouting?" said the cow. "I'm not deaf."

"Someone reported seeing something unusual," said Biskit, lowering his voice.

"Yes, my name is Mavis. I made the report."

"And what is it you think you've seen, Mavis?" asked Biskit.

"Think? I don't think I've seen something, I *have* seen something."

"All right. Then what have you seen?" he said, trying to be patient.

"Dung, deary."

"Dung?" repeated Biskit.

"Yes, I'm a dung spotter. It's my hobby."

"A dung spotter?"

"Why do you keep repeating everything

I say?" Mavis asked, waving a fly away from her backside with her tail. "Are *you* deaf? Is that why you were shouting?"

"I was shouting because..." Biskit realized he was shouting again. Cows were so infuriating. "Never mind. So you've spotted some dung in a field of cows. And that's strange because...?"

"It appeared overnight, twelve dollops of dung in a circle. Under the old willow tree in the far corner of the field."

"A dung circle?"

"Yes, come on. I'll show you."

Biskit followed Mavis through the field. It was dotted with cowpats of all shapes and sizes, from the freshly dropped sloppy ones to those so old they had grown a skin. Biskit did his best to avoid them, but Mavis marched straight through.

"Doesn't anyone ever clean up around here?" asked Biskit.

"Clean up?" said Mavis. "It's good for the soil. Did you know dung is full of nutrients?"

"How fascinating," said Biskit, sounding anything but fascinated.

"Dung is a very interesting subject, you know," said Mavis. "I've got over fifty names for the different types. That one over there with all the flies? I call that a swirly plop. And that one you just stood in – I call that a squelchy stinker."

Biskit wiped his paw on the grass.

Mavis stopped in a brittle old cowpat that snapped like a biscuit beneath her hoof and nodded across the field. "There's the tree. Your mice friends are up there," she said. "Good luck, Agent Biskit. And I hope your hearing improves."

"I'm not d… Oh, what's the point!" Biskit hated cows.

CHAPTER 4

THE DUNG CIRCLE

The Nothington Extra-terrestrial Research Division (NERD, for short) was made up of a team of mice led by their super-intelligent leader, Example One. They had all been lab mice once, but Example One had been given a brain-growing drug that turned him into a genius overnight. The only side effect was that it had made his fur go pink. Biskit sometimes wondered why he didn't invent something to turn it white again. Also, if he was so smart, why had he named his department NERD?

"Morning, Nerds," said Biskit.

The white mice busily scurrying
between cowpats paused to look at him.

"Ah, Agent Biskit." Example One peered
at Biskit through his wire-rimmed spectacles.
"Have you seen this? It's most intriguing. It
appears to be some kind of extra-terrestrial
waste product. Notice the regular positioning."

Biskit looked at the twelve identical cowpats
arranged like numbers on a clock face.
He sniffed one. It smelled nasty.

"Alien dung?"
he said.

A cold wind made him shiver and he wished he was inside a warm cinema picking popcorn off the patterned carpet, listening to the exciting soundtrack of *Danger Dog*.

"Unexplained alien poo. If my calculations are correct, then…" Example One tapped at the miniature computer tablet he was holding with a stylus. It came on for a moment then beeped and shut down. "Out of battery again!" he said. Example One turned to the other mice. "Example Four, were you playing games on my tablet again last night?"

"It weren't me, boss," replied a white mouse. "It was Example Twelve."

"I don't care who it was. Get me a new one." Example One pulled out the dead battery and lobbed it at the white mouse. The mouse ducked and the battery flew over his head then landed in the middle of one of the cowpats with a **SQUELCH!** It sank down into the brown gunk and immediately the whole thing began to vibrate.

"How interesting," said Example One.

The cowpat fizzled with purple sparks then suddenly rose up into the air, revealing what appeared to be a metal base with flickering lights.

"Look at that. Flying dung," said Example One.

"It's a *Poo*-F.O.," Biskit sniggered.

The cowpat flew around in a circle, sending purple sparks from its metal base. The other eleven cowpats joined it. They got faster and faster until suddenly they all collided. A great burst of purple electricity flashed as the cowpats fused together and crashed to the ground.

The other mice scurried away in fear but Biskit and Example One peered at the large metal egg-shaped object now lying still on the grass.

"How remarkable," said Example One.

"Keep back." Biskit placed his paw on the mouse's tail.

"Honestly, you field agents." Example One tugged his tail free. "You always assume everything in the universe is out to attack us. I wonder what—"

Example One's words were interrupted by another purple spark as a crack appeared in the egg's surface. The metal shell fell away, revealing a beetle-like creature about the size of a small dog. Its body was dark brown and it had glassy round eyes. When it brought its pincers together, electrical sparks flew.

"How intriguing." Example One approached the beetle. "It appears to be some kind of alien beetle formed of waste product."

Biskit turned to address the creature. "Well, you alien dung beetle, it's time to turn around and go back to where you came from."

Biskit could see his face reflected in the beetle's eyes. He stood with his paws firmly on the ground, lowered his head and let out a threatening growl.

The beetle made a noise that sounded like **scrickerty-tick-tick** then suddenly darted forwards. It ran straight under Biskit's legs and scurried down the field at great speed.

Biskit gave chase. This time there was no sidestepping the cowpats. He ran straight through them, sending bits of dung flying all over the place. The beetle reached the stone wall at the edge of the field and began to scramble up and over the jagged stones.

Biskit came to a halt in the middle of an especially gooey cowpat. On the other side of that wall was the cliff. The very thought of it made his legs go weak, but Biskit had a job to do. He hopped up on to the wall and peered over the cliff, taking in the sheer drop and the pebbly beach far below. The beetle had landed on the beach without injury and now it seemed to be heading in a straight line towards the town.

Biskit felt queasy. He felt faint. It wasn't falling he was afraid of – it was landing that worried him. But Biskit knew that whatever the alien dung beetle was up to, he had to stop it.

He jumped.

CHAPTER 5

HAVOC IN THE CINEMA

Jumping off a cliff was not the silliest thing Biskit
had ever done. It was not even in the top ten
silly things. But as the wind whistled through
his flapping ears, he did wonder if it would be
the last silly thing he did. Biskit aimed for a large
rock pool and hoped it was wide enough and
deep enough to break his fall. He spread his legs,
closed his eyes and bellyflopped into the water.

WHA-SPLA-BOOOSH!

"YEEOOOOWW!"

The pain was incredible. The water was freezing. Biskit felt barnacles scrape his belly, but there was no time to stop and inspect his wounds. The beetle was still moving speedily over the pebbly beach towards the town. It came across a washed-up tin can, which it snatched up in its pincers then gulped down, sending purple sparks flying. Biskit stepped out of the rock pool, shook himself dry and took off after the beetle. At least the water had washed away most of the dung.

The beach was empty, but there were a few humans up on the promenade and the beetle was heading straight towards them. Biskit ran as fast as he could but even though he gained on it a little, the dung beetle had reached the promenade before he was at the stone steps. Biskit bounded up the steps in time to see the beetle scuttling across the road.

A car swerved and the driver shouted, "Hey, watch it!" but the beetle kept on going, straight into the path of a rubbish cart.

"What on Earth…" the road sweeper started.

"Witness," woofed Biskit at the top of his voice.

The road sweeper turned to look at the barking dog. "Who do you think you're barking at?"

The beetle seemed unaware of the man staring at it and the dog chasing it. It simply carried on, over the rubbish cart, across the pavement and through a door.

"Hey, that's the cinem—" Before the road sweeper could finish his sentence, something wet and sticky landed on his head. "Eurgh, that's disgust—"

As the Forget-Me-Plop took effect, the man forgot what he was saying. He forgot about the beetle and about the dog. He looked down at his broom in confusion, trying to remember what he had been doing. Something white, gooey and nasty dripped on to his nose. "Pesky birds." He pulled out a tissue to wipe his head and entirely forgot what he was about to say.

Biskit followed the beetle into the building. Nothington Cinema was Biskit's favourite place in the world: the smell of the popcorn, the ketchup stains on the carpet and the thrill of the movies. But he wasn't there to see a film. As Biskit's eyes got used to the dark, he saw the beetle run over someone's foot.

"What was that?" The man leaped up in surprise and threw a fizzy drink into the air. It rained down on the rest of his row, who immediately jumped to their feet. Popcorn, snacks and drinks were thrown up, causing a chain reaction until every single human in the cinema was shouting. Meanwhile, the beetle that had caused all the fuss had already gone.

Biskit followed it along a corridor and down into the foyer where a couple of ushers stood, looking thoroughly bored until an unusually large brown beetle skittered by, closely pursued by a scruffy brown dog.

CHAPTER 6

MITZY THE CAT

As Biskit chased the alien dung beetle across the high street, he heard the cries of confused humans suddenly silenced by the **SPLATS**, **SPLOTS** and **SQUERCHI-SPLUPS** of Forget-Me-Plop raining down on their heads.

A seagull swooped down over Biskit's head. The speaker on its leg crackled and Biskit heard Commander F's voice. "Biskit, you dopey dog! What the limp lettuce leaf is going on?"

"I'm kind of busy right now, sir," replied Biskit.

"Busy causing chaos! Yes, I'm watching the whole thing on the seagull cameras."

"Couldn't we talk about this later, sir?"
Biskit panted.

"No, we can't! Agent Biskit, I've no other
choice but to send in—"

A screech of skidding tyres cut short the
conversation. The seagull flew out of the way
of the car while Biskit executed a perfectly
timed forward roll, then dived away from the
path of an oncoming motorbike.

Biskit had no time to stop and check
everyone was all right. The beetle was now
scuttling through a supermarket car park.
He knew the only way to stop the alien
creature would be to get in front of it and
trap it somehow. He leaped over the car park
wall, skidded across the bonnet of a car and
somersaulted straight off it. It would have been
a spectacular move had his face not gone smack
into the wire mesh of a supermarket trolley.

"Argh! My shopping!" yelled the elderly man,

watching the trolley spin out of his hands.

Biskit picked himself up and barked by way of apology, but he couldn't afford to lose sight of the beetle. He gave the trolley a push in the direction the beetle was heading and, as it picked up speed, he jumped in. He heard the **GRUH-CRUNCH** of twelve large eggs breaking and the **SPLA-FLOSH** of a carton of fruit juice exploding, but the trolley gave him just enough of a boost to catch up with the beetle. As he drew alongside it he threw his weight to one side, tipping the trolley over in an attempt to block its path. He missed. Instead the trolley slammed into the side of a car, setting off the alarm.

Biskit groaned. His head throbbed, but he couldn't stop. He hadn't trapped the beetle, but he had knocked it off course. Now it was heading towards a large glass-recycling bin. Biskit realized that the beetle's route would take it straight into the bin, up its side then in through the hole where the bottles usually went. All he had to do was jam a couple of bottles into the hole to prevent the beetle from getting out.

Unfortunately, his front right paw had taken the brunt of the fall and he was barely able to keep up, never mind overtake it. The beetle **CLATTER-CLUNKED** into the bin and scrambled up its side, just as Biskit had predicted. It slipped into the bottle slot and dropped inside, but Biskit was still too far away to make it secure.

Hobbling as fast as he could, Biskit made for the bin. Then, as if from nowhere, a cat appeared on top holding an empty bottle between her teeth and another with her tail. The cat looked at Biskit pointedly then jammed the bottles into the gap, capturing the beetle inside.

"You're welcome," purred the cat. She was a tabby with white paws and a white patch over her nose. She arched her back and meowed.

"Who are you?" Biskit snarled. He could hear the beetle scrabbling against the metal sides of the bin.

"The name's Mitzy."

"Well, Mitzy, as much as I appreciate your help, I've got this under control."

"Really?" said Mitzy. "Looks to me like you just allowed an unidentified alien threat to cross a civilian area."

"What's it got to do with a granny cat, anyway?" demanded Biskit.

"Don't call me that," hissed Mitzy.

A seagull landed next to the cat and the speaker around its leg crackled to life.

"Good work, Agent Mitzy," came the voice of Commander F.

"Thank you, sir," she replied.

"*Agent* Mitzy?" said Biskit. "But ... *what*? She works for the Pet Defenders?"

"Agent Mitzy is new to the team," said Commander F. "Her owner has just moved here to retire by the sea."

"That's right," said the cat.

"So you are a granny cat," said Biskit. "Pampered, soft, never done a hard day's work in your life. Yep. I know your kind."

"You don't know me." Mitzy scraped a claw along the top of the bin. It made a **SKRIIIIIINT** noise that made Biskit shudder.

"Stay off my case." Biskit growled.

"Oh, I can see you two are going to get

on like a hutch on fire," said Commander F. "Biskit, this is your new partner."

"But … but … she's a cat," said Biskit.

"I don't care if she's a duck-billed platypus! She's your new partner and you both need to keep that beetle contained until the NERDS can identify what it is. Do you understand?"

CHAPTER 7

A BITE TOO FAR

Biskit didn't like cats and he certainly didn't want a new partner. So having a cat assigned as his new partner was the worst thing he could imagine. Biskit settled down in front of the bin and flopped his ears over his eyes. Perhaps if he ignored her for long enough, she'd take the hint and leave.

Mitzy jumped down and landed by his side.

"Come on," she purred. "If we're going to be partners, we'll have to find a way to work together."

"I don't work with cats."

"Why not?" asked Mitzy.

"I don't trust them."

"There are as many cat agents as dog agents."

"It's not about that. Cats are disloyal. You're never content with one owner. I've seen you lot running from house to house, going wherever you can beg a bowl of milk or a tin of salmon. Dogs aren't like that. One owner is enough for us."

"Not all cats are alike." Mitzy sat down and licked her paw then rubbed her ear. "You heard what the commander said. We're partners. We need to work together. We need to trust each other."

"I don't trust you and you'd be crazy to trust me. I'm too unpredictable. I do silly things and, as Commander F will tell you, I never think before I act."

"I know," said Mitzy. "You've been following that thing all morning and never once have you stopped to come up with a plan to actually catch it."

Biskit stood up angrily. "If you don't like how I do things, why would you even agree to be my partner?"

"Because you've also stopped more attacks than any other agent in this division ... possibly in the whole organization. You are willing to do anything to catch your target. Even if it involves jumping off a cliff in broad daylight." Biskit tried not to smile. "So you're either very brave or very stupid."

"Maybe I'm both," said Biskit. "Either way, I don't need a partner."

"Yes, you do." Mitzy began cleaning her hind legs.

"Do you have to do that?" asked Biskit.

"At least we cats do clean ourselves."

"I have baths," said Biskit defensively. "I had one last month … or the one before."

Mitzy continued cleaning her fur. "Besides, I always do this when I'm thinking about a case."

"It's not your case to think about," stated Biskit.

"Someone has to. That beetle has been on the move since it cracked out of the dung egg. The question is, where's it going?"

The bin rattled.

"Wherever it was going, it's not going there any more," said Biskit.

There was a **CLANK!** and a dent appeared in the side of the bin.

"It's trying to get out," said Mitzy.

"Come on," barked Biskit.

The Pet Defenders scrambled up the side of the bin as the whole thing began to shake.

CLA-DONK!

"We need to weigh it down," said Biskit.

CLA-BA-DONK!

The noise had drawn the attention of the shoppers. They stared as one of the recycling bins tipped over, flinging a scruffy dog and a tabby cat off it. With a **KRA-DANGK!** the top flew off and a huge beetle appeared.

It was now about five times bigger than when it had entered the bin. The shoppers yelled in terror and stared in disbelief. A shop assistant pushing a line of shopping trolleys collided with the wall. Some people reached for their camera phones. But before any photos were taken, something white, gooey and disgusting **SPLATTED** on their heads.

The beetle made a **scrickerty-tick-tick** sound and snapped its pincers together, making purple sparks fly. Biskit and Mitzy approached the creature.

"Welcome to Planet Earth." Mitzy looked up at the beetle's large glassy eyes. "It is our job to defend it. If you come in peace, we ask that you leave in peace."

The beetle titled its head, but said nothing.

"I think you're wasting your time," said Biskit. "It doesn't understand!"

"We need to find out what it wants," said Mitzy. "We might be able to find a way of getting it off our planet without resorting to—"

Before Mitzy could get any further, the beetle ran at her, catching her off guard and pinning her down. She struggled but the beetle pressed at her throat with its pincers. She hissed angrily and wriggled, trying to get free.

"Let … her… go," snarled Biskit.

The beetle squeezed its pincers around Mitzy's throat.

Biskit leaped forwards and sank his teeth into the beetle's back leg. It let out a pained **scrickerty-tick-tick** then spun round, releasing Mitzy and turning its attention to Biskit. He could see the whites of his teeth reflected in its eyes.

"Listen, you big ugly space bug, I don't care if you can understand me or not," he snarled. "This is not your planet. It's time to leave."

The beetle snapped its pincers at Biskit and small purple sparks flew off them. Biskit dodged the attack but the beetle came at him again. This time the pincers caught his tail and Biskit felt a sharp electrical shock surge through his body.

Then everything went black.

CHAPTER 8

THE SECRET LAB

Biskit often dreamed he was floating through space. In reality, he had never left Earth, but in his dreams he had been among the stars a hundred times or more. He was happily drifting through the endless nothingness when he heard Commander F's voice out of the darkness.

"How long has he been out?"

"Two hours," came the reply. It was Mitzy.

"So what happened? The gull cameras went offline. Doing something silly, was he?"

Biskit opened one eye, but used his ear to shield it from the dazzling overhead light.

"He was saving my life," said Mitzy.

Commander F grunted. "Well, two hours is long enough." Biskit felt a sharp jab in his side. "Get up."

"Ow." Biskit raised his ear and rolled over.

He was in a room with white walls and scientific equipment on the shelves. It was Example One's Alien Research Lab. It had been a lab for human scientists until the super-intelligent mouse had hacked into the computers, fired them all and taken over. Mitzy and Commander F stared at him.

"You're all right?" said Mitzy, unable to hide the relief in her voice.

Commander F removed the fat carrot from his mouth and said, "Of course he's all right."

"So where's the dung beetle?" asked Biskit. His back made an alarming snapping noise as he stretched.

"It got away," said Mitzy.

"Got away where?" asked Biskit.

"It ran off in the same direction it was heading before we trapped it."

"You should have followed it," said Biskit.

"Yes, she should have," said Commander F. "Instead she decided to help her useless partner and drag him all the way to this lab while he was still dangerously infected with live alien electricity."

Biskit noticed that Mitzy's fur was singed and patchy.

"Thanks," he muttered. "I'll say this. You're pretty tough for a granny cat."

"I told you not to call me that," Mitzy hissed, her hair standing on end.

"Enough bickering, you two," said Commander F. "Our priority right now is to find this beetle. We have every agent on the ground and in the air searching for it but, so far, nothing."

The door slid open and Example One

scurried in, carrying his tablet under one arm and the stylus in his mouth. "Ah, Biskit. Back with us, eh? Fascinating stuff, that alien electricity. Could have been very nasty for you had your partner not brought you here so quickly."

"She's not my partner," said Biskit.

"Never mind that," said Commander F. "We need to find this beetle and send it packing."

"Well, I've run a full analysis on the samples we picked up in the field, trying to identify it," replied the pink mouse.

"And?" said Commander F.

"Nothing." Example One tapped the side of his head three times then slipped the stylus behind his ear.

"Nothing!" exclaimed Commander F.

"Whatever it is, it has never been here before. Isn't that wonderful! A new alien life form. A new problem to solve."

"I don't like problems," said Commander F. "I like solutions. Agents Biskit and Mitzy, I think it's time you took a trip to the vet."

Biskit groaned. This day just kept getting worse.

CHAPTER 9

A VISIT TO THE VET

Philip loved his dog very much, so he was disappointed to find that Biskit had run off that morning. He'd been looking forward to their trip to the cinema together. He knew it was silly. Biskit was a dog. How could he be expected to remember anything? Still, Philip had spent the day waiting for him to return and when Biskit did slope back in through the dog flap, he had a limp.

"Oh dear," said Philip. "Is that leg giving you trouble again?"

Biskit nodded his head weakly and tried to

take a step towards Philip. As he put his weight on his front right leg, he dipped and let out a pained moan.

"I think we'd better take you to see Doctor Udall."

Biskit whined and flopped to the ground, apparently too weak to lift himself.

Philip picked him up and rubbed his face into the back of Biskit's neck.

Biskit felt bad about deceiving his owner, but he had no choice. In the middle of the day, the easiest way to see the vet was to take his owner.

"We'll get you something nice to snack on for the journey, shall we?" said Philip. "A couple of those Bark Bites you like?"

"**Woof! Woof! Woof! Woof!**"

To Philip it almost sounded as though Biskit was saying, "Sounds good to me," but that would have been ridiculous.

Biskit felt less bad as he sat on the back
seat munching Bark Bites and listening to
Philip's attempts at singing along with the
radio. In fact, he enjoyed the journey so much
that he almost forgot his limp on the way in
to the vet's.

Inside the waiting room a miserable-looking
receptionist sat under a parrot cage. There
was a poorly Pekinese, an off-colour golden
retriever, a black cat with a bad cough and an
extremely elderly hamster in a clear plastic
ball. Their owners all sat on chairs discussing
what was wrong with their pets, while the
animals were on the floor, grumbling among
themselves.

Biskit kept his head down. He didn't want
to listen to them moaning. He had just had
several million volts of alien electricity run
through his body and you didn't hear him
complaining.

61

Philip gave his name to the receptionist.

"There's a bit of a wait," she said.

"I don't mind," said Philip. "My dog's very important to me."

"Aren't they all," she said flatly.

"Feed the fish!" squawked the parrot. "Feed the fish!"

"Quiet down, you." The receptionist

scowled at the bird then turned back to Philip.
"Please take a seat."

The door behind her opened and a middle-aged woman appeared. "Philip, please come in."

"Some of us have been waiting a long time," a lady protested.

"That's right," barked the Pekinese.

"Philip's dog is a special case." Dr Udall turned to Philip. "Is it Biskit's leg again?"

"Yes." Philip looked around apologetically as he carried Biskit inside.

Dr Udall closed the door behind them and Philip placed Biskit down gently.

"Now, let's have a look at this…"

Mmmmm-Ziizzzz!

A strange shimmering filled the room and both humans stopped moving as though someone had pressed pause.

"Wow. That's cool," said Mitzy, pushing the

window open and jumping into the room.

"I thought you were going to wait outside," said Biskit.

"Partners stick together," she said firmly. "What's happened to the humans?"

"If you must know, they've got the stares," he replied.

"The stares?" repeated Mitzy, taking a closer look at the unmoving vet.

"A State of Time and Reality Experience Suspension," said a low female voice.

Mitzy looked around to find who had spoken, but all she could see was a murky fish bowl.

A goldfish appeared out of the gloom and pushed itself up against the glass.

The voice came again, deep and echoing, and Mitzy realized that it was the goldfish who had spoken.

"Being able to suspend time and reality is one of the perks of being such a vastly superior species. Although I wouldn't expect such primitive life forms as yourselves to understand it," said the fish. "I can control their minds like puppets on a string."

"Or fish on a line," said Mitzy, licking her lips.

"I may look like a fish to you," said the fish, "but I am actually a super-intelligent multi-dimensional being. And I can do a lot more than talk."

The fish flapped her left fin and swam upwards. But it wasn't just her that moved. The water poured up and out of its container, gradually arranging itself into the same shape as the bowl, only without the glass. The fish remained at the centre and the whole thing floated down until it was level with Biskit's head.

"Mitzy, meet Barb. Barb, this is Mitzy," said Biskit.

"Who is she, Biskit?" asked the fish.

"I'm his new partner," said Mitzy.

Bubbles appeared as Barb laughed. "New partner, eh?" she said.

"Commander F's orders," snarled Biskit.

Barb winked at Mitzy, taking her by surprise. She'd never seen a fish wink before.

"Don't mind him," said Barb. "He still hasn't forgiven himself for losing his last partner."

Biskit growled. "I did everything I could to save Champ," he said.

"See what I mean," said Barb, with a low chuckle that created ripples on the surface of the sphere of water. "Don't worry. He's not as grumpy as he makes out."

CHAPTER 10

THE DUNG GUZZLER

Mitzy didn't know what was more amazing: the two humans frozen in the middle of the room or the fish hovering inside the floating water.

"So, Biskit, I assume you're here because you need my help," said Barb. "That's usually why you agents come to me, because you have something you're struggling to understand."

Biskit decided to let it go. Barb was the most annoying fish he had ever met, but she was also the smartest being on the planet. And she was right — he did need her help. "We have a creature we need to identify," said Biskit.

"Bring it out, then," said the fish.

"We lost it." Biskit looked pointedly at Mitzy. "But we know what it looks like. It began as twelve cowpats, then it became an egg that hatched into a kind of beetle thing—"

"With a kind of purple electrical current," added Mitzy.

"I was getting to that," said Biskit, glaring at Mitzy.

Barb sighed. "All right. Let's see…" She blinked twice, making the room go dark. Twinkling stars appeared from within the gloom.

"What's going on?" asked Mitzy, looking around.

"I have travelled to every corner of the universe," said Barb. "I have visited a trillion planets. I keep my memories so that I may help simpler species, such as yourselves."

"Is she always like this?" whispered Mitzy.

"This is her on a good day," replied Biskit.

The stars swirled around the room and
rearranged themselves into the shape of a large
creature with six legs and two long antennae
jutting from its head. "This is the Gargantuan
Guzzle Snuffler, from the seventh moon
of Snob-Dobble Chops,"
said Barb.

"Nope," said Biskit.
"Ours didn't have the
things sticking up."

"Very well."
The stars rearranged
themselves again, this time into the shape
of a creature with a large bulbous bottom.
"The Bottopotamus of the Bomping Flex
quadrant," said Barb.

"That isn't ours
either," said Mitzy.

The stars shifted
again, forming

various different creatures — each one as weird
and wonderful as the last.

Mitzy and Biskit dismissed them one by one
until a beetle appeared with pincers and round
glassy eyes.

"That's the one,"
said Biskit.

"Ah, a Dung Guzzler
of the former star
Dun-Glowing," said Barb.
"Are you sure?"

"Yes," said Mitzy.

Biskit and Mitzy peered at the image of the beetle.

"The Dung Guzzler is one of the most destructive pests in the universe," said Barb. "It is born out of waste product and it feeds on rubbish. It favours discarded electrical goods but, as it grows larger, it becomes less fussy. Eventually, it will eat any old rubbish."

"A rubbish-eating alien doesn't sound so bad," said Biskit. "Might tidy up this planet."

"Unfortunately not," said Barb. "You see, they soon grow so large that they trample entire buildings, towns and cities, reducing them all to rubble. They don't just feed on rubbish. They make it." As she spoke, the swirling stars formed shapes that illustrated her words. The image of the alien beetle consumed imaginary buildings. "Once everything has been laid to waste and all that waste has been consumed, the only thing left for it to eat is the planet itself. Of course by that point, the planet is little more than a massive lump of rubbish floating through space."

"You mean if we leave this thing long enough, it'll eat our entire planet?" said Mitzy.

"Precisely." Barb flicked her fin and the sphere of floating water drifted across the room and poured back into the bowl.

Mitzy, who had watched the light show with an increasing sense of panic, said, "You seem very calm about this." She sprang up on to the windowsill.

Barb swam round her bowl. "To me, my dear, Earth is just one small planet in a very big universe. I have seen Dung Guzzlers lay far bigger, more important and better defended planets to waste."

"We'll stop it," said Biskit between gritted teeth.

Barb pushed her face up to the side of the bowl, making her eyes seem even larger. "Then you have no time to lose. With a good supply of rubbish, a Dung Guzzler will grow impossibly big within a matter of hours. Good luck, Pet Defenders. You'll need it."

Barb blinked once, and suddenly Philip and Dr Udall were released from their trance.

"… this leg then," said Doctor Udall.

"Yes, it's the front right one," said Philip.

They were unaware that anything out of the ordinary had happened, but they couldn't fail to notice Biskit jumping out of the window after a tabby cat with white paws.

"Biskit!" yelled Philip.

Biskit felt bad running out on Philip again, but what could he do? The world needed his help.

CHAPTER 11

THE DUMP

The road sweeper lifted his broom off his trusty cart with a sigh. He had lost count of how many birds had pooped on him that day. He was looking forward to a nice cup of tea and a sit down, but first he had to deal with the litter outside the fast-food restaurant. He had just swept all the empty cartons and burger boxes into a big pile when a shaggy brown dog ran straight through it.

"Hey!" he cried.

A tabby cat came next, darting through the middle and messing up his pile even more.

"Oi!" he yelled.

He pondered how unusual it was for a cat to be chasing a dog, but the thought vanished when he felt something splat on his head. In a matter of seconds he had forgotten all about it.

Biskit and Mitzy stopped in an alleyway alongside a Chinese restaurant. It smelled good. Biskit could almost taste the sweet and sour sauce. He sniffed at a bin and a black cat jumped up, startled. The cat hissed at him then ran away.

Biskit smiled at Mitzy. "Street cats are always so jumpy," he said.

"You scared her," said Mitzy.

"So what? She's only a scavenger." Biskit sniffed the box of noodles the black cat had been eating then took a bite. "Mm, nice. Could do with more soy sauce though."

"If she's a scavenger, what are you?" snapped Mitzy.

Biskit gulped down the noodles. "I'm a dog with a job … and I work better on a full stomach."

"Never mind your stomach. We need to find that beetle before it destroys the world," said Mitzy.

"You worry too much." Biskit spoke with his mouth full. "We've got agents all over town looking for it and Barb will get word to the NERDs in case they can help. It's only a matter of time before we catch that purple-powered pest. And when we do, *I'm* going to need the energy to defeat it." Biskit swallowed a half-eaten spring roll.

"We," said Mitzy firmly.

"I'd rather you didn't while I'm eating," joked Biskit.

Mitzy didn't smile. "We're supposed to be working as a tea—" She stopped mid sentence. "Biskit, that's it. Energy. You're not the only one who needs energy." She licked a paw and wiped her nose. "That's what it's after, too. The beetle is hungry! Barb said that it starts off feeding on electrical items."

"I suppose that explains why it came to life when that mouse's tablet fell in the dung," said Biskit. "But how does that help us find it?"

"It seems like it's been heading somewhere specific. Somewhere we'll find a load of old electrical…" Mitzy's eyes lit up. "I've got it! I know where it's going."

"Where?" said Biskit.

"The town dump. It's full of old fridges, cookers and televisions."

"Of course! The dump!" Biskit wondered why he hadn't thought of that. He took another mouthful of noodles then ran to the end of the alley. "Let's go."

"No. This way," said Mitzy. "I know a shortcut."

Like all towns, Nothington-on-Sea was full of routes that were out of sight of its human inhabitants. Mitzy led the way as they crossed gardens, zipped down alleys, hopped over walls and crawled through holes in fences. She even knew the best spot to get in through the large metal fence. Biskit didn't stop to wonder how Mitzy knew the route so well.

Inside the dump were huge containers for different types of waste. Right in the middle was a mound of old electrical items. A man in a yellow hard hat operated a giant claw, which he used to move items of rubbish into the correct places.

"I can't see any sign of the beetle," said Biskit.

"It will be down there somewhere. I know it. We need to dig," said Mitzy.

"That could take hours," replied Biskit.

"Not if we borrow that."

Biskit looked at the huge mechanical claw. He hated to admit it, but Mitzy was right. It was the quickest way of searching the area.

CHAPTER 12

THE CLAW

The claw operator enjoyed his job at the town dump. He liked lifting and dropping the rubbish into different piles. The heavy stuff was best – the **CLANK-KANGGG!** of a radiator or the **KER-CHA-DONNNGGGG!** of a cooker. He was having a relaxing day up until the moment when a cat landed in front of him with a hiss and a dog leaped up and slammed his paws on the door, barking.

"ARRGHH! WHA-A-AH!" The claw operator jumped up in fright, whacking his head on the top of the small cabin. "AA-OWW!"

He lurched to the side, the door flew open and he fell out.

"Should we check that he's all right?" asked Mitzy as she and Biskit jumped up into the cabin of the claw machine.

"He'll be fine," said Biskit. "Most of those seagulls up there are just scavengers, but there'll be some of ours, too. If he needs it, Commander F will send one down with a medi-kit."

"You shouldn't use that word," Mitzy said sharply. Her eyes flashed with anger.

"Medi-kit?"

"Scavenger. Just because they don't get tins of food emptied into bowls with their names on, it doesn't make them less important than you."

"That's true," sniggered Biskit. "Me being more important than them makes them less important than me. Now, watch and learn."

Biskit jumped up on to the control panel and pushed one of the levers, but he couldn't quite reach the other. The mechanical arm swung round and smashed a cooker against the side of a skip.

DAH-SMOOU-CRUNCH.

Bits of glass and metal flew all over the place.

Mitzy hopped up on to the seat. "We need to work as a team to make this thing dig," she said.

"I'll get the hang of it in a minute." Biskit scrabbled around on the dashboard, sending the claw into a garden-waste container then out again, clutching a huge bunch of brambles between its metal teeth.

"No, you won't," said Mitzy. "You need to do as I say."

"You? I'm in charge here."

"Yes, but I know how this thing works. Now, you take the lever that moves the claw, I'll work the one that opens and closes it."

Mitzy jumped on to the control panel and took the end of the right lever in her mouth.

Once again, Biskit realized she was right. Working together was the only way of making the claw do what they wanted. Slowly but surely, they dug a hole in the pile of rubbish until Mitzy cried, "Stop. Look."

"What?"

"Something moved."

"I can't see anything but rubbish."

"Look, there by that broken sofa!"

The pile of rubbish was moving ever so slightly, as though something beneath the surface was breathing.

Mitzy and Biskit swung the claw over to the spot.

"Ready?" said Mitzy. "One, two…"

"Three." Biskit plunged the metal jaws into the ground.

Scrickerty-tick-tick.

They tried to raise the claw, but it was jammed. Whatever it had between its jaws was big enough to hold it there.

"Keep pulling," said Biskit.

"This whole thing will fall apart if we do," said Mitzy as the machine vibrated with the strain. "We've got to release it!"

"No. Look. It's coming up," replied Biskit.

Slowly the beetle emerged, dragged out by the claw's grip on its back. It was now the size of a small car.

It slipped out of the claw's grasp and hit the ground.

THU-DUH-DUMP THU-DUH-DUMP!

It scuttled round in a circle then began digging with its pincers and throwing piles of rubbish into its mouth. Purple electrical sparks flew and the rubbish sizzled with energy. A radio came on, blasting out a pop song until the beetle devoured it in one bite.

"We need to stop it burrowing down again," said Mitzy.

"Leave it to me," said Biskit. "Can you work this claw on your own?"

"I don't think I could do any worse than you," replied Mitzy, curling her tail around the other controller. "What are you going to do?"

"I'm going to distract it so that you have time to pick up the heaviest object you can and drop it on that Dung Guzzler's head."

"It's too dangerous. Look at the size of it! You survived once, but do you really think you'll live if it gets you in its pincers this time?"

"Not thinking things through is what I do best," Biskit replied. "Now, let's crush this beetle."

CHAPTER 13

THE TRUTH ABOUT MITZY

While Mitzy did her best to control the claw, Biskit jumped out of the cabin window. He hit the ground in a forward roll, then landed on a rusty old tray. He skidded into a pile of stinking bin bags that burst and sprayed him with sticky brown bin juice. Shaking off as much gunk as he could, he edged forwards, and stepped straight into an empty baked beans can. As he twisted round to pull his paw free, his back legs got tangled up in a plastic bag and he tumbled over. Finally, he bit through the plastic and headed towards the beetle, which was devouring rubbish fast.

"Hey! Dung for brains!" barked Biskit. "What's the rush? Why don't you hang around?"

The beetle didn't even stop to look at him.

Biskit leaped forwards and sunk his teeth into the beetle's back leg. The creature let out an angry **scrickerty-tick-tick** and twisted around, bashing Biskit's head into the side of a large metal barrel.

Biskit collapsed to the ground. The round glassy eyes were now even bigger than before. Biskit felt dizzy. He tried to get up, but slipped and lost his footing.

Scrickerty-tick-tick.

The beetle reared up on its back legs, opening and closing its pincers. Bright purple sparks flew as they connected. They were bigger, louder and more deadly than before. And now it had him in his sights.

Biskit stared up at the terrifying creature. Beyond it, he could see the seagulls circling in the blue sky. Commander F would be watching from the safety of his HQ, noting all the mistakes Biskit made in his final moments. What did it matter? It was all over now.

Or was it?

Suddenly a large white object loomed into view. Biskit looked up. A huge freezer dangled between two metal claws.

"Get out of the way!" yelled Mitzy.

Up in the control cabin, she couldn't tell whether her partner had heard her, but she knew what she had to do. She opened the claw and dropped the freezer, right on to the beetle's back. It landed with such force that it drove the beetle down into the ground in a mass of fizzing, hissing confusion.

"Biskit?" She leaped out of the cabin and staggered over the mounds of rubbish. "Biskit!" She ran round the beetle. "Bis…" The scruffy brown dog was lying motionless on the ground. He was bashed, bruised and burnt.

"Biskit?" She nudged his belly with her nose.

"Ow," he said.

"Biskit," she sighed.

"Good shot." He said weakly. He tried to lift his head, and failed.

"Thank you," said Mitzy. "I guess it's not so bad having a partner after all. Right?"

93

"You got lucky this time, but nothing's changed," said Biskit. "I don't want a partner."

"I just saved your life," protested Mitzy.

"I work alone." Biskit staggered to his feet and inspected his wounds.

Mitzy stood directly in front of him, forcing him to meet her gaze.

"What?" he said.

"I understand that it's not easy. Losing a partner, I mean. You can't blame yourself."

Biskit lowered his head and closed his eyes for a moment, then opened them and looked at Mitzy. "Champ was a good dog." He spoke quietly. "Not the best agent, but a good dog… A family dog. Loyal. The kind that gets included in the family photos." Biskit gritted his teeth. "One mistake and he ended up the wrong side of the universe. His family is left thinking he ran away."

"It's for their own good," said Mitzy.

"Is it?" demanded Biskit. "Is it better that Champ's family believe their beloved dog ran out on them because we have to protect them from the truth."

"It wasn't your fault," said Mitzy.

"You don't know what it's like to lose someone."

"Don't I?" Mitzy's green eyes burned with ferocity.

"You lost a partner, too?" said Biskit.

"Not my partner. My owner… I *was* a granny cat, but one day I came home. No owner."

"So where do you live now?" said Biskit. "Who feeds you?"

"I sleep wherever I can. I eat whatever I can find. I'm what you like to call a street cat. I'm a scavenger. Why do you think I know this dump so well? I spent three nights here when I first arrived in Nothington."

"So how come you moved here in the first place?" asked Biskit.

"I came to look for my owner. She used to talk about this place. I thought I could find her, but I've checked all the nursing homes. She's not here."

"Does Commander F know all this?"

"No."

"So you lied?"

Mitzy looked away, ashamed. "You know as

well as I do – pets don't trust strays. Never have. I was the same. Only when it happens to you do you understand that strays are just animals."

A seagull landed on the rim of a bathtub. The speaker around its leg crackled and they heard Commander F's voice. "Well done, Defenders, you stopped that thing. Example One is on his way over to help clear up the mess. Most impressive, both of you."

Before either of them could respond, there was a **RUMBLING**, a **CRUMBLING**, a **CRUNCHING** and a **SCRUNCHING**, as the piles of rubbish shifted beneath their paws.

The beetle was moving.

Scrickerty-tick-tick.

The seagull spread its wings and took flight.

"What's happening?" they heard Commander F's voice cry.

With a **KAR-RUNCH** and a **SCH-MAAASH!** the beetle threw the freezer off its back.

The Pet Defenders dived out of the way
as it came crashing to the ground. The beetle
raised its head and brought its pincers together,
squeezing the freezer in its deadly grip. Huge
purple sparks flew and the beetle tipped its
head back to devour it in one enormous gulp.

"Agent Mitzy! Agent Biskit! What the rotting
radishes is going on?" yelled Commander F.
"I've lost visual contact."

"It's time for round
two," said Biskit.

CHAPTER 14

ROUND TWO

The beetle grew larger with every piece of rubbish it consumed. Within a matter of minutes it was the size of a house, with pincers as big as elephant tusks.

"Any ideas?" asked Biskit.

"We could drop something even bigger on it," suggested Mitzy.

Mitzy started towards the mechanical claw, but the beetle beat her to it with a couple of giant steps. It brought its pincers together and crushed the cabin. Glass sprayed out as the windows shattered and bolts of purple

electricity **FIZZLED** and **CRACKLED** as the beetle
yanked the cabin off its base and tossed it in
the air.

The seagulls kept their distance, while the beetle continued to feed.

The claw operator lay motionless on the ground.

"We need to get that thing away from the human," said Mitzy.

"Hey, you big lumbering pile of junk, you overgrown trash-eating insect, you massive muck-munching monster," yelled Biskit. "What about us?"

Scrickerty-tick-tick.

The beetle swung its head round. Its huge glassy eyes were the size of dustbin lids now. It swung its pincers, but Mitzy ducked and Biskit dived, both expertly avoiding its attack. Sparks flew from the pincers, hitting old electrical items and bringing them to life. A toaster popped. A microwave pinged. A kettle exploded.

Scrickerty-tick-tick.

The beetle took another swing at Biskit. This time he skidded out of the way on a take-away box then took cover behind a broken old sofa. He found Mitzy crouching on a cushion, shielding herself from the electrical surges.

"Did you see how it brought all that old stuff to life with its electrical current? Maybe there's some way we can overload it or cause a short circuit," said Mitzy.

"It's worth a go," said Biskit.

KARRRUNCH!

The beetle sliced the sofa in two. Biskit rolled out of the way as it took a huge bite from a matching armchair.

"There's a skip full of old computer equipment over there," said Mitzy, pointing to one that was overflowing with broken computers, photocopiers and printers.

"We need to make sure it follows us," said Biskit.

"I don't think that'll be a problem," said Mitzy.

The beetle was close behind as they ran towards the skip. They had no hope of outrunning it, so instead they weaved in and out of its legs, avoiding its jabs and lunges. When they reached the skip, Biskit and Mitzy scrambled up the side.

"Come on, then, you great big bin-biter," yelled Biskit.

"Yeah, give it your best shot!" cried Mitzy.

Screckerty-teck-teck.

The beetle sounded angry. It towered over them, waving its pincers.

Just as it brought its pincers together, both Pet Defenders jumped off the other side of the skip, out of its reach. Instead of grasping Mitzy and Biskit, the beetle had dug its pincers right inside the skip. The charge lit up the sky like a fireworks display. Circuit boards fizzled, printers started printing, photocopiers started

103

photocopying and computers blew up.

Scrickerty-teck-taack!

The beetle recoiled as plastic and metal flew into the air.

Biskit could only watch in horror as a massive old computer monitor plummeted towards Mitzy. "MITZY!" he yelled.

She turned to face him, but it was too late. With a **SMA-CRAASH** the monitor landed on top of her.

For a split second, Biskit forgot about the beetle and the sizzling electrical items. He didn't care about anything except his partner. Blood pumped in his ears as he ran towards her. He staggered, slid and slipped on the rubbish beneath his feet, but nothing was going to stop him. When he reached her, he rammed his shoulder against the monitor.

The monitor toppled over, revealing Mitzy curled up inside. It was hollow.

"Are you OK?" said Biskit, trying to hide his relief.

"Yes, I think so. Did it work?" asked Mitzy.

Scrackerty-tack-tack.

"Of course not," said a squeaky voice.

They looked up to see a pink bespectacled mouse riding a seagull.

CHAPTER 15

EATING BISKIT

Example One patted the seagull's neck as it landed on the rubbish heap, then reached into a saddlebag and pulled out a soggy chip, which he threw in the air. The seagull tipped his head back and caught the chip in his beak before gobbling it down whole.

"What an absolutely fascinating creature this Dung Guzzler is turning out to be," said Example One.

"Yes, fascinating." Biskit dodged pieces of rubbish raining down. "How do we stop it?"

"It's an interesting question. I have been

mulling it over since our first encounter with
the beetle," said Example One.

The beetle took a huge bite from a
television set, sending bright sparks flying as it
BUH-GUN-CHEW-RUNCHED through it.

"I think mulling time might be over," said
Biskit.

Example One hopped off the seagull, then retrieved the stylus from behind his ear and looked down at his tablet. He seemed completely unconcerned about the ever-growing beetle beside them. Finally he tapped the stylus against the side of his head.

"It appears that the electrical current flowing through the Dung Guzzler is what allows it to grow so rapidly. It's also a good form of self-defence."

"You don't say," said Biskit.

"Yes, I do," said Example One. "Mitzy had the right idea about its electrical current being the key to defeating it."

Scraackerty-tack-tack.

The sound the beetle made became deeper as it grew to the size of a church.

"So how do we stop it?" shouted Mitzy and Biskit as one.

Example One blinked, adjusted his glasses

and slipped the stylus behind his ear. He
reached into the seagull's saddlebag and pulled
out something that looked like a marble.

"With this," he said.

"What is it?" asked Mitzy.

"It causes a brief but powerful
electromagnetic surge. If my calculations are
correct – which they usually are – when I turn
it on, it should knock out the beetle's electrical
current for up to three minutes."

"What good will that do?" asked Biskit.

"I'm hoping that without its electrical power,
it will return to its original state…" He paused.
"Of course, it's impossible to be sure."

The beetle reared up on its back legs
and then landed back down with a

THUDDER-CHUDDDER-BOOOFFF!

It turned its magnificent head to look at the
Pet Defenders. Its eyes looked like two glass
moons looming down at them.

"What are you waiting for, then?" said Biskit.

"Well… It needs to be activated from inside the beetle," said Example One. "I can turn it on remotely, but you need to get that thing to eat it."

"No problem," said Biskit confidently. "Leave it to me."

"Watch out!" cried Mitzy. She pushed Example One sideways, saving him from an enormous pincer, but knocking the marble out of his hands.

Biskit raced after the marble as it flew through the air. He was aiming to snatch it between his teeth, but he slipped on a mouldy yoghurt pot as he reached it and ended up swallowing the marble whole.

Mitzy rushed over. "Did you get it?"

"Ye-es," replied Biskit hesitantly.

"Great, because we need to stop that thing before it gets any bigger."

The beetle was munching a flat-screen television like it was nothing more than a wafer-thin mint.

"There is one problem," admitted Biskit, scratching his ear with his hind leg. "I swallowed it."

"You swallowed it!" exclaimed Mitzy. "Maybe Example One has another."

But Example One was struggling to keep his seagull under control as it tried to flee the huge monster.

"Don't worry," said Biskit. "Just make sure you give it time to digest me before Example One activates it."

"Digest you? What are you going to do?" exclaimed Mitzy.

Biskit smiled. "Something I haven't thought through."

"You don't need to think through getting eaten by a giant alien beetle to know it's a bad idea. You'll never survive."

"If I don't, I need you to do something for me," said Biskit. "I need you to make sure Philip is all right. I'm all he's got."

Mitzy looked at her foolish, brave partner. "I'll make sure he's OK, I promise. Now you be a good dog and come back."

Biskit smiled, turned and bounded towards the beetle.

Scroockerty-toock-tooock.

As the beetle began to open its jaws, Biskit

took a step back. He spotted Example One standing on the back of a sofa, watching, and he could hear the cries of the seagulls circling above, transmitting every detail to Commander F. Biskit looked at Mitzy and winked.

"On behalf of the Pet Defenders," he said, "welcome to Planet Earth. It is our job to defend it. If you come in peace, we ask that you leave in peace. If you do not come in peace, we will escort you out."

Scrockerty-toock-tooock!

Biskit shut his eyes as the creature's gaping mouth closed around him.

CHAPTER 16

*

CLEARING UP THE RUBBISH

"Now, Example One. Activate it NOW!" Mitzy yelled.

Example One gave the thumbs up, then tapped his stylus on the tablet.

Instantly they heard a strange rumbling sound as the beetle rocked back then tipped over. Purple energy bolts crackled like lightning around his body and it let out an agonized scream.

SCREEEKETY-TEEEKK-TEEEKK!

It tried to rise up but three of its legs became dislodged. It rocked over and the

other three snapped off. It brought its pincers
together but this time, instead of sending
sparks flying, they crunched into each other and
smashed to fragments. The beetle was falling
apart piece by piece.

Example One joined Mitzy. He scribbled
something down on his tablet. "It does appear to
be working entirely according to my theory…"

His words were cut short by an almighty

KAA-SPLA-BOOOOM!

as what remained of the beetle exploded.

Mitzy dived on top of Example One to shield him from the raining rubbish.

Once the worst of it was over she looked up. There was a huge blackened crater where the beetle had stood.

"Excuse me," said a muffled voice from under her belly.

"Sorry, Example One." Mitzy stood up and the pink mouse crawled out.

"That's the first time I've been grateful for a cat pouncing on me," he said.

Mitzy couldn't bring herself to smile. "Where's Biskit?"

Example One climbed up on to the long handle of a vacuum cleaner. "I can't see him just yet. But look, our beetle has returned to its original state!"

In the centre of the crater were twelve cowpats in a circle, but Mitzy didn't care about that right now. She leaped over them, shouting, "Biskit! Biskit!"

Tap, tap…

The sound came from an upside-down barbecue.

"Biskit?" Mitzy pushed the barbecue over to reveal a dog with scruffy brown hair and big floppy ears. His fur was singed at the ends. Patches of it had burned away altogether. Little purple sparks flew from his teeth as he smiled and staggered to his feet.

"This … doesn't … change…" was all he managed before he collapsed to the ground.

"I know you don't want a partner," said Mitzy. "But you've got one, so live with it."

Meanwhile, Example One was examining

the twelve cowpats. "We'll have to keep these apart if we are to analyze them safely," he said.

"Never mind that," said Mitzy. "Is Biskit going to be all right?"

Example One looked at the Pet Defenders agent over the top of his spectacles. "He'll be fine. Just a few bruises, but apart from that…"

A seagull landed next to them and Commander F's voice spoke.

"Nice work, Pet Defenders," he said. "Our clear-up team will take it from here. You can have the rest of the day off, Agent Mitzy."

"What about Biskit?" Mitzy looked at her partner, slumped on the ground.

"A gull will be down with a medi-kit shortly. We'll get him cleaned up and back home," said Commander F. "I expect you have a home you want to get back to, too."

"Yes, sir." Mitzy tried not to think about what quiet corner of the town she would find to sleep in tonight. "Biskit was very brave, sir."

"Or very foolish," said Commander F.

"I think he was probably both," said Mitzy. "Luckily for us."

Biskit woke to find himself in the familiar surroundings of his dog basket. He couldn't see the clock, but it was dark outside. He could hear Philip snoring, which meant that his basket had been moved into the bedroom. Biskit liked it when his owner did that. He yawned and snuggled into his blanket.

He flopped his ears over his eyes, hoping he could drift into his floaty space dream. He had no idea what had happened back at the dump, but Earth was still spinning, which meant that he had done his job. He had defended it. The only reward he wanted was a good night's sleep. He yawned.

He could feel himself drifting off to sleep, floating up into space, when he heard a *tap, tap, tap* at the window…

Read an extract from

The Leaky Battery Sets Sail

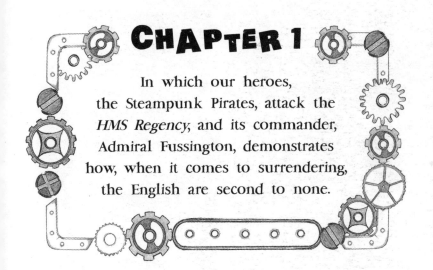

CHAPTER 1

In which our heroes,
the Steampunk Pirates, attack the
HMS Regency, and its commander,
Admiral Fussington, demonstrates
how, when it comes to surrendering,
the English are second to none.

At first glance, there was nothing especially remarkable about the pirate ship that emerged from the thick sea mist and drew alongside the *HMS Regency*. Its billowing sails were white. Its flapping flag was black. Its crew of ragged buccaneers jeered and cheered and waved their razor-sharp cutlasses as their captain cried, "Surrender, you English mummy's boys or we'll fire up the cannons and blast more holes in your ship than you'll find in a barrel full of Dutch cheese, so we will."

However, these were no ordinary pirates. Under the captain's dark blue hat was a face made of metal that glinted in the sunlight. Steam shot out of his ears and his head. He wore a heavy woollen coat, open at the front to reveal a clock on his chest. It had only one hand that was madly whizzing around.

"Oh no, it's the *Leaky Battery*!" cried the

terrified lookout on the *HMS Regency*. "It's Captain Clockheart and the Steampunk Pirates!"

Captain Clockheart laughed. "You hear that, First Mate Mainspring? Load up the cannons."

"**Click**, aye. **Tick**, aye. **Tock**, Captain," replied a pirate with a bowler hat, chequered trousers and a large key slowly rotating in the middle of his back.

"We surrender!" Admiral Fussington immediately raised his hands.

"Load 'em up and prepare to... Hold on. Did you say *surrender*?"

"Yes! Don't fire – we give up." Admiral Fussington turned to his crew. "Sergeant Thudchump, order your soldiers to lower their weapons."

The sergeant motioned to the rest of the crew and they reluctantly put down their guns.

The hand on the captain's clock suddenly stopped and steam *put-put-putted* out of his head in confusion. "I don't understand."

"Och. Let's blast 'em to smithereens. Surrendering is no way to stop us attacking," snarled Mr Gadge, who wore a tartan kilt and bandana to match, and had a hook in place of his left hand. He twisted his arm and the hook was replaced with a cannon ramrod.

"Hold your fire, Gadge," said the captain. "I'd like to know why a ship of the Royal Navy would surrender so quickly."

A mechanical bird with a few colourful feathers glued to its wings landed on his shoulder and squawked, "A bunch of scaredy cats!"

"How rude. Not at all," protested Admiral Fussington. "I'm simply following the latest guidelines with regards to P.C.S.s."

"Ah, ignore Twitter," said Captain

Clockheart. "What's a P.C.S. when it's at home?"

"A potential conflict situation. The rules now state that senior officers should immediately surrender. Look, I've got a kit and everything." The admiral opened a bag and pulled out a stick with a white flag wrapped around it. After carefully reading the instructions, he unfurled the flag and gave it a little wave.

Captain Clockheart laughed then turned to the rest of his crew, who joined in, their mechanical jaws clanking and clinking.

"Right, you lot," yelled the captain. "First Mate Mainspring, lower the boarding planks. Gadge, Loose-screw, Blind Bob Bolt and the rest of you merciless metallic marauders ... PREPARE TO BOARD!"

ABOUT THE AUTHOR

Gareth P. Jones

Gareth is the author of many
books for children, including the
Ninja Meerkats series, *The Thornthwaite
Inheritance* and *The Considine Curse* (Blue
Peter Book of the Year 2012). He and his
wife Lisa are allergic to most pets. Instead
they keep two children, Herbie and Autumn.

Find out more at www.garethwrites.co.uk

ABOUT THE ILLUSTRATOR

Steve May

Steve was born by the sea in sunny
Hastings. He once dreamed of becoming
a pop star but instead he studied
illustration and animation. His madcap and
action-packed style has become a regular
feature in the world of children's books.

Find out more at www.stevemay.biz